BOOKS BY ELIE WIESEL

the G

OLEM

The Story of a Legend

as told by ELIE WIESEL

and illustrated by MARK PODWAL

Translated by ANNE BORCHARDT

SUMMIT BOOKS · NEW YORK

Published by SUMMIT BOOKS
A Division of Simon & Schuster, Inc.
Simon & Schuster Building
1230 Avenue of the Americas
New York, New York 10020
SUMMIT BOOKS and colophon
are trademarks of Simon & Schuster, Inc.
Designed by Edith Fowler
Manufactured in the United States of America

10 9 8 7 6 5 4 3 2 1

Library of Congress Cataloging in Publication Data

Wiesel, Elie, date
  The Golem.

    1. Golem. 2. Judah Loew ben Bezalel, ca. 1525–
1609—Fiction. I. Title.
PQ2683.I32G6 1983   [Fic]   83-9304
ISBN 0-671-45483-8
        0-671-49624-7 deluxe edition

For our sons
Elisha Wiesel
and
Michael Podwal

THE GOLEM

The Story of a Legend

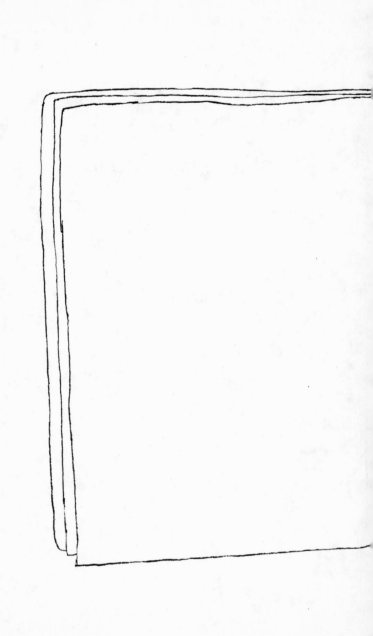

I OWE this legend to an old beggar named Shmaike. He was a cripple, yet, for some reason we called him "Shmaike the tall one." A strange man, he would remain silent throughout the entire year and begin to talk only during the week preceding Passover. Then he would tell only one story —always the same story—which he allegedly inherited from his uncle, an idle bachelor whom no one took seriously. This uncle had been told the story by his maternal grandfather, Rebbe Issachar, a true scholar who had attributed it to his Master, the famous Rebbe Ephraim, who was said to have possessed the powers of the Maharal, the celebrated Wonder Rebbe of Prague, but to have refused to use them for fear of blundering. And also because he claimed that the Lord, blessed be His name, ought to save our people without intermediaries.

Rebbe Ephraim had heard the tale from a gravedigger, Reuven, son of Yaakov, who claimed to have witnessed the numerous miracles that legend attributes to the Golem, the most fascinating creature in Jewish lore and fantasy.

And now, surely you would like to hear the story of the Golem. Let Reuven tell you here and now: I truly liked him, and I was not the only one. We loved him. To us he was a savior. Though mute and unhappy, a savior is what he was. Nobody understood him because no one was like him. Do you know anyone who lives only for others, who devotes his every breath, his every thought, every inch of his being to a single, sacred purpose: to protect the life, the security and the future of the community? He was said to be a fool, I know. They said he was stupid, backward. I do not agree. He was a saint. May I burn in hell if I am lying. What I am telling you is the truth. As a member of the Holy Brotherhood, I know the fragility of life and the power of death; I know that they are separated by the most tenuous thread. Is it not the same for what is true and what is false?

So listen to me carefully: I, Reuven, son of Yaakov, declare under oath that "Yossel the mute" or the "Golem made of clay," created in the year 1580 by the great and famous Rabbi Yehuda Lowe of Prague, known as the Maharal, blessed be his memory, deserves to be remembered by our people, our persecuted and assassinated and yet immortal people. We owe it to him to evoke his fate with love and gratitude.

You must understand: if I tell you that the Golem because of his duties and achievements, was a fully accomplished being, it is because it is true. And we miss him. More than ever, we need his presence and perhaps even his mystery. As usual the year promises to be one of punishment; I feel it in every bone of my body. I have lived through too many ordeals not to be able to predict what the future has in store. Oh, of course, I have faith in God: I would not be a Jew if I did not have faith. But neither would I be a Jew if I were not afraid. What can I say? I read the signs and I know how to interpret them; I am used to them. On the

13

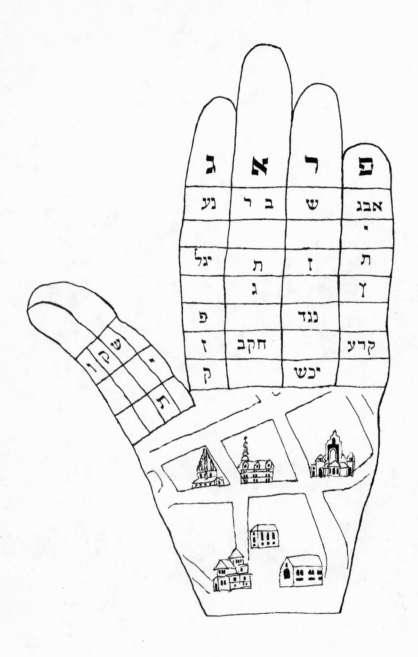

face of death, on the table of purification, where the members of the Holy Brotherhood prepare men for burial, I sometimes read not the past but what the past breeds. I know that sometimes there are men who choose death because they wish to escape this wretched earth, which first bears us but then devours us.

Ah, if only the Golem were still among us . . . I would sleep more peacefully. Why did the Maharal take him from us? Did he really believe that the era of suffering and injustice was a thing of the past? That we no longer needed a protector, a shield? Tell me, please: our Maharal who knew everything, did he not know that exile, after him, would become harder than before, even more cruel? That the burden would become heavier, more bloody? He could have left us his Golem; he should have. What did he fear? A religious movement that would have turned the Golem into an idol? Our "Yossel the mute" was really mute. He would not have dreamed of turning us away from the path that leads to God. On the contrary. . . . But then why did he have to return to dust? Certainly all men are mortal, but the Golem was different, you know that. If you want my opinion, the

"Golem made of clay" was immortal, as immortal as the hatred he was asked to fight. Today, as yesterday, someone must stand between that hatred and us. If only the "Golem made of clay" could come back to life. None other could prevent the spilling of blood; none other could disarm the murderers and conquer evil.

He was a savior, I tell you.

I remember: I was ten or eleven, or perhaps a little older; we were living in the tiniest of alleys in the Jewish quarter of Prague. We were poor, but I was not aware of it. For the Shabbat, we always had blazing candles, fish; my father seemed happy and my mother seven times more so. Father was always happy, or at least he always seemed to be. At night, he sang while working at the bakery; during the day, stroking his beard, he studied the Talmud, with a faraway look in his eyes. I really loved my father.

One day—it was the beginning of spring—when I looked at him, he seemed unusually sad, but I could not understand why. We were getting ready to celebrate the joyous feast of Passover. "Why do you look so unhappy?" I asked him. He seemed not to have heard me. I repeated my question. He sighed and said gently, "You cannot understand yet."

Worried, I insisted; he evaded my question. "You are too young," he said, trying to reassure me. "You will grow up, you will understand." I eventually discovered why he was so sad. A week before Easter, our entire community was plunged into anguish: we were expecting a massacre. Why? What a question! Do our enemies need to justify, with specific reasons, why they thirst for Jewish blood? This time they had prepared everything: they had hidden the body of a Christian child in the cellar of Shmuel the merchant; as a result we were accused of having performed a ritual murder. It was said that we needed Christian blood to make matzos. Such idiots! Their viciousness equals their ignorance. Our Scripture says and our Wise Men repeat, and our Masters have proven that ever since Jews have been Jews, they have never committed this kind of crime. Ritual murders have no place in the Jewish tradition. Even Abraham did not carry out his deed; his son survived the ordeals imposed on him by his father.

Twenty years before, all the Hebrew books in Prague were seized and taken to Vienna where they were examined for such a ritual. Not even a single prayer book was left behind, and the cantor had to chant the prayers from memory. Two years later the books were finally returned. For us, all life is sacred; the great Maharal succeeded in convincing Cardinal Sylvester himself—and he was the head of the church in Prague. And King Rudolph too—and he was our ruler. You will not find an

intelligent person, a sensitive person, who will give credence to these dark, ugly rumors. And yet, there are those who continue to secretly spread such lies with only one purpose: to stir up hatred, to provoke violence and the shedding of Jewish blood.

Of course, we turned to the Maharal: wasn't he our guide, our spiritual leader, a model of wisdom and courage? Of course, he did his best to explain to the authorities that Shmuel the merchant was a just and charitable man; he vouched for his innocence. Nothing helped. They arrested the merchant and his whole family. His youngest son, Yehoshua, my classmate, also was arrested. I remember his face, or rather the fear in his face. "Don't be afraid," the Maharal told them in a strong, calm voice. "God knows that you have done nothing wrong and what God knows, others

will learn also." We accompanied the prisoners all the way to the Christian district where, at the foot of the turreted wall, a howling mob was waiting for us, screaming threats and obscenities. In spite of the noise, I could hear the clatter of chains. But I could no longer see my friend Yehoshua and I felt as if I had somehow betrayed him. The merchant and his family vanished into a courtyard and I wondered if I would ever see them again. I was so anguished by this question that I could hardly breathe. Then the Maharal turned to us and said, "Let us all go to the synagogue; let us join our prayers with those of our unfortunate brothers. God will hear us, I promise you."

Slowly, very slowly, the men and the women —my father and my mother also—started walking toward the synagogue that dominated the small square in our quarter; and I, one of the youngest, ran off ahead.

How I loved and will always love this synagogue which is unlike any other. It is called "Alt-neue shul"—the old-new synagogue—but it also means "Al-T'nai" or "on condition" (that one day we shall give it back to Jerusalem). Our ancestors built the shul two thousand years ago, after the

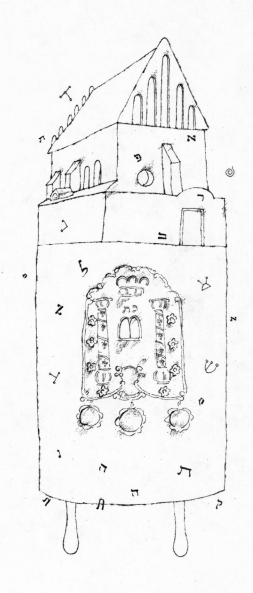

dispersion of Judea and the destruction of Jerusalem. It is said that angels in heaven carried away
stones from the Temple and set them into the
beautiful building, which is still the pride of our
community. The old synagogue had survived
many catastrophes. When my father's father was a
boy a huge fire broke out in the Jewish quarter.
Only the synagogue remained untouched. On its
stepped gable sat two mysterious white doves, and
there they remained while the fire raged through
the ghetto. Neither the flames nor the suffocating
smoke could drive them away. After all danger to
the Altneue shul had passed, the two doves vanished. At night we avoided going near the synagogue. It was rumored that all the dead met there
to pray and study, in their own way—and to remember. Only the Maharal would go there day or
night. He was never afraid.

BUT now the great synagogue was overflowing. We recited psalms for hours and hours, first sobbing, then whispering. The candles flickered, the voices shook. Our strength was abandoning us and so was the light. At one point after dark the Maharal stole away, followed by his son-in-law, Reb Yitzhak, son of Shimshon Hacohen. Curious by nature, I sneaked outside. I saw them going toward the Rabbinical Court House. I was trembling and shivering with cold. I had to make an effort to prevent my teeth from chattering, but I was determined not to return to the warm shelter. Because of the darkness, I was able to come close to the Maharal and his son-in-law without being seen. They entered the dark Court House, and like a shadow, I followed them. They

headed for the hearth where "Yossel the mute" usually slept. The Maharal shook him gently, affectionately, and said to him with a tenderness which moved me then and astounds me even now, "You have not done your work, dear little Yossel; you let an enemy pass, carrying the body of a Christian child in his pack; and now may God have pity on us all." The Golem, crushed, opened his eyes wide and made a gesture of regret; he was asking for forgiveness. The Maharal touched his shoulder and continued, "It isn't too late, my dear little Yossel. As long as man is alive, all remains possible. We have a week. We must solve the mystery before the first Seder. You can do it, can't you? Surely you can do it?" The Golem nodded his head several times. Yes, he promised to do it. "You will succeed, my dear little Yossel, because you have never failed before; it is God's will that you thwart the fatal plans of our enemies. I have confidence in you, my dear little Yossel."

Then he gave him precise instructions: Scour the neighboring cemeteries and search for an empty grave, since the enemy had undoubtedly removed from its grave a child who had just died. By identifying the child, the Golem would unmask

those who had defiled the grave. Can you imagine what followed? The Golem went out into the night and began to roam the cemeteries. He finally found the empty grave. How? Not limited by his senses, he could see souls and not just their bodies. And, as everyone knows, the soul likes to hover about the body it has just abandoned. The Golem noticed the soul of a child that seemed in deeper mourning than the others. When told, the Maharal called for the police. They opened the grave. Someone remembered having seen two peasants wandering nearby, during the night. Someone else added that the two peasants had sworn revenge on the Jewish merchant, to whom they owed five hundred crowns. They were questioned; they broke down. That year the Jews of Prague celebrated Passover with more joy than ever.

Let me tell you, we do need the Golem.

What did he look like? You would like a portrait. In your own mind he looks like a monster. You imagine him excessively tall, strong, heavy, dragging his body like lead—some kind of human beast that nature put on earth to mock or frighten it. Well, let me tell you, you are mistaken. I, who have seen him in my childhood, I remember him

31

perfectly; it is as if he were standing in front of me now. I can see him more clearly than I can see you. He was somewhat taller than the Maharal, who was very tall, and somewhat heavier. His bearing was awkward and yet astonishingly agile. Riveted to the ground, but floating in the air. Strange, mysterious, he seemed to plow earth and heaven all at once. Sure of himself, he moved ahead inexorably. Nothing could stand in his way. Without pity for the wicked, fierce toward our enemies, he was charitable and generous with us. I should add that he was blessed with both intuition and intelligence. On the street you would have turned to look at him, not because of his appearance but because of something else, and I do not know what; he radiated a force which overwhelmed you, moved you, flooded you with emotion.

The most striking thing about him was the way he looked at you; he could penetrate the very recesses of your memory, as if he were searching for his own. His eyes, dark and huge, devoured yours. Sometimes those eyes burned, when he wanted to make a point or to reassure; at other times they looked dull, resigned. But even more striking was his shadow, which followed the Ma-

haral's as if refusing to let go; sometimes in the street at night or in the enchanted forest, the two shadows would unite for a second and you could feel them living a life of their own which filled you with terror. Separated, the two men, the two shadows, would move away and disappear. When we looked around for the Golem, he was gone; he was already at his usual place in the Court House, asleep.

Since he never talked, and since he always seemed to surprise you, to shock you, to force you out of the ordinary, to break your habits, some people would get impatient with him. But he, like a sleeping or walking statue, exhibited total indifference. Almost unapproachable, he allowed no one to offend him. If he was ridiculed, he ignored it. If stones were thrown at him, he did not react. There was almost no way of getting him angry. Only the godless enraged him; his brothers could do anything.

In spite of what you think, he was not less human than we, but more human.

UT now I must stop a moment to tell you of his creator, the great Maharal. I knew him also. What I mean is I saw, heard, observed, followed, loved him. As a child I longed to be near him. I knew I would learn things from him, things only he could teach. He would lead me on invisible paths, he would show me miracles like those Moses had performed long ago: In his very small house with only two rooms, he could accommodate four hundred disciples.

The great Rabbi Yehuda Lowe, the Maharal. The only one. Can we say enough about his eloquence, his gifts? Thanks to him, we all lived in very special times. Let me recall his life and his work for the children of Israel. It is symbolic that even his birth is tied to a legend.

35

Passover 1513: the family of the renowned Rabbi Bezalel ben Hayyim of Worms is gathered around the dining room table, reciting with fervor and joy the story of the exodus from Egypt. They are singing, they are praying, proud to belong to this people thirsting for freedom; then they eat and drink, raise high their wineglasses to toast the Prophet Elijah, who, on that night, visits all the Jewish families throughout the world so he can participate in their happiness and their vigil. In the next room the Rabbi's wife starts to moan: her labor pains are becoming more and more agonizing. At midnight, the very moment when her husband is reciting the verse *Vaiehi bakhatzot halaila*—"And at midnight"—the child is born, and it is a boy, destined to become the Maharal. At the same time a stranger approaches the house carrying a bundle on his shoulders. Frightened by the infant's cry, he runs away. The police arrest him and discover the body of a dead Christian child in his bag. He confesses everything: some distinguished citizens had paid him well to hide the dead child in the Rabbi's house. The Jews of Worms will never forget that they owe their salvation to the Rabbi's son: his birth coincided with the defeat of their enemies. He was named after the Kabbalist Reb Yehuda Lowe, also of Prague, whose tombstone states that he belonged to the royal line of David.

Later, Rabbi Lowe himself left Worms to study in Prague. His life spanned the sixteenth century from beginning to end. He married Pearl, the daughter of Rabbi Shmelke Reich, when he was thirty-two and she was twenty-eight. They had six daughters and one son. He died at the age of ninety-seven, leaving behind him profound and erudite works covering every aspect of Jewish life, and a legend that consoles the hunted, the persecuted. Even today, I only have to think of him and I feel better.

Very tall, erect, majestic, he inspired respect and obedience. There was something about him which made you speak softly. No one dared meet his gaze; he represented a celestial power without name. It was said that King Rudolph treated him as an equal; I certainly believe it. In his own way, the Maharal was king, that is, he imposed his will on others—not to be different from them, but to show them the way to follow, the words to say or not say. After he died, even Christians would visit his grave to place bits of paper into the crevices of his tombstone in the hope that he would intercede on their behalf in heaven.

Legends about his powers and self-sacrifices are too numerous to count or even to recall. He once stood for hours and hours on the Charles Bridge of Prague, waiting for King Rudolph's golden carriage to pass. Onlookers threw stones at him but they might as well have been flowers. In fact, they were changed to flowers. One man asked him, "Why do you stand here?" "I must speak to the king," he answered. "But the king may arrive in ten hours, or fourteen"—"Well, I shall wait until he arrives." "But how can you be sure he will agree to hear you? He may not even stop here. Usually, his horses run faster than the wind." "Not this time," said the Maharal. The people went on sneering at him until the royal carriage was in sight. The horses came running as though to trample the Rabbi under their feet . . . and then, suddenly, they stopped. The Maharal approached the carriage and greeted the king. "Why did you risk your life?" asked the king. "I had to," said the Maharal. "My people's lives are in jeopardy. Have you not signed a decree ordering them to go into exile?" The King invited the Maharal to join him. 39

Together they went to the royal Hradcany castle. From then on the Maharal became a frequent visitor in the role of intercessor and defender.

An eloquent speaker, defender of his people in disputes with representatives of the Christian world, he liked to retire alone to his study and read the Talmud and the Zohar, the ancient laws and their more recent interpretations. He seldom laughed, and he smiled only when playing with his adored granddaughter Eva. He loved her with all his heart. She was so beautiful; she was good and obedient, and her thirst for knowledge and the knowledge she acquired were astonishing. She read the Bible. And Rashi. And the Midrash. With her, the Maharal was always patient and gentle.

He is known to have become angry only once. He was old, very old. One evening, when he returned alone to the great synagogue, the Angel of Death was writing the names of his future victims on a long scroll. Our Rabbi grabbed it from him, went back home and threw it into the fire. But a piece of parchment remained in the Angel's hand. With one name on it: our beloved Master's. He passed away a week later.

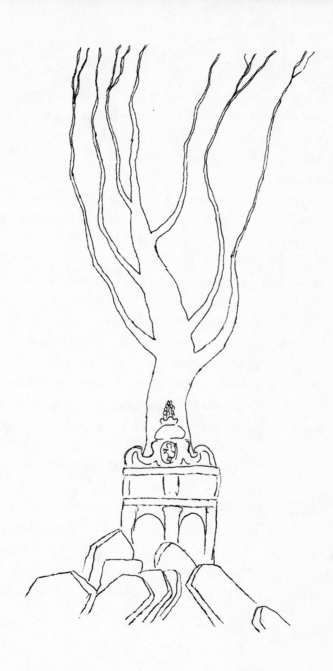

Why did he not send his Yossele to battle the Angel of Death? Because Jewish law counsels us to oppose violence and bloodshed with words and prayers rather than with more violence and bloodshed? Does not the Torah allow man to kill the killer in self-defense? Are we not told every Passover eve that, at the end, God himself will slaughter the Angel of Death? Why are we to wait that long? Why didn't the Maharal make Yossele immortal so he could vanquish Death then and there? Was it out of pity for his "Yossel the mute"? Possibly. The Maharal loved him—oh yes, he loved him deeply. He loved him too much to inflict upon him the curse of being the eternal survivor. In this case, Yossele's own welfare was of importance to the Maharal. I am sure that ultimately the Maharal saw in Yossele more than an instrument—a friend, and perhaps much more than that.

And that is how he was with "Yossel the mute." Whenever he pronounced his name, or his nickname, Yossele, his voice rang with tenderness and affection. You would have concluded that he wanted to help him, although it was the "Golem made of clay" who was supposed to help *him*, the Maharal, and us too—since times were inauspi-

cious, filled with difficult and disheartening ordeals.

What the Lord does, man must accept. Even if it hurts? Especially when it hurts. And it did hurt, it hurt very much to see so many men tortured, so many women mourning, so many terrified children. But you bowed your head and blessed the heavens; you could do nothing else.

But the Maharal, attuned to the suffering of his congregation, refused to submit to cruelty. Impotent before the immensity of evil, he chose to question the world above. Using mystical rituals into which he had been initiated, he formulated the question he wanted to ask in a dream. And the answer came hidden in the first ten letters of the alphabet of the sacred tongue. For everything is in the word; it is enough to arrange certain syllables, to form certain sentences, speak certain words according to a defined rhythm, to be able to lay claim to celestial powers and master them. The Maharal knew where to look and what names to invoke. From above he was told that to save his people he must create a new being: the "Golem made of clay" would answer fear with fear, unjust violence with

just violence. Like the evildoers, he would stay

awake nights—but to fight them, to expose their plots. He would be given every means to unmask the bloody-handed, sneering killers.

Yes, the Maharal, in his wisdom, had understood: the society in which the Jews lived, terrified of the future, had fallen so low that only a Golem —an artificial being without a soul, a creature of clay, dedicated to earthly matters and excluded from divine inspiration—could still have an effect and save it from perdition. That is why the heavenly answer given to the Maharal in his dream contained only ten letters from the Aleph-bet: they were sufficient to create the Golem, or at least to project him into the world. If the message had contained all twenty-two letters, it would have meant that a perfect being was needed.

The Maharal, blessed be his memory, went to work. And from then on nothing was the same.

ONLY one person witnessed the scene, and only from a distance. He understood nothing. Too frightened to think or to stop thinking, he felt paralyzed, unable to move, to breathe, to look or not to look; he even forgot that he was alive. He was like a Golem waiting for the Maharal in order to be born into the world.

It was only later, by way of rumors which circulated secretly through the Jewish families of Prague and of the neighboring villages, that visions and memories formed a whole picture. Bits of sentences from a famished old man. A glance from the Maharal's beadle, Reb Avraham Hayim; a sigh from Rabbi Yitzhak Hacohen; everyone possessed a fragment of a tale; they had to be brought together to create a legend.

On that day, the twentieth day of Adar, 1580, the great Rabbi Lowe summoned his two favorite disciples to his study: his son-in-law Rabbi Yitzhak Hacohen and Rabbi Sasson. After swearing them to secrecy, he told them of his dream, of the revelation and his decision. He reassured them when they were unable to suppress a cry of astonishment: it is not the first time that a Golem would have been created, he explained. In the Talmud, a sage named Rava had done it before.

But there had also been many, many attempts that had failed. When Rabbi Ishmael ben Elisha, with his students, tried to fashion a Golem, the earth swallowed them. Our lawmakers even had had to answer some of the questions raised by the presence of such a creature: Could it be included in a minyan? There are books, procedures, formulas at the disposal of the initiated. "Don't be frightened," the Maharal added. "No one will do anything here on earth if it is not commanded from above; we only translate divine thoughts into human terms."

Then he gave them books to study in depth, litanies to repeat with a particular fervor, and he advised them to fast, to remain pure, during seven

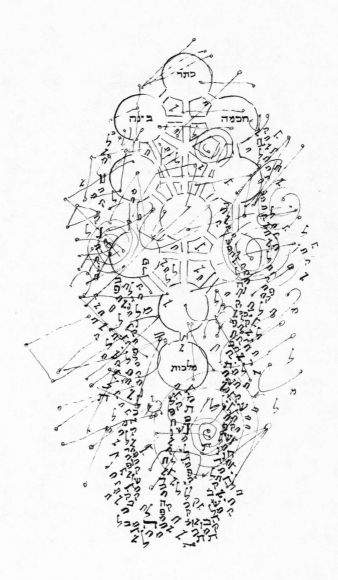

days and seven nights. Afterward they were to immerse themselves in the ritual baths, get dressed, and return to his study at four in the morning, with their shawls and phylacteries and prayer books.

They arrived at the appointed hour, shaking with cold and fear. In the ominous semidarkness they saw the Maharal with a finger on his lips; the silence was not to be made impure by words. He then proceeded to speak through gestures; they were to imitate him faithfully, do everything he did. They left the Court House and found themselves in the dark and threatening street. The Maharal took a deep breath and raised his cane to indicate the direction. Wordlessly, they left the silent Jewish quarter and made their way through the wider streets of the wealthy Christians. They headed toward the woods along the outskirts, near the Vltava river. The Maharal stopped at a certain place, scrutinized the sky, then the damp ground, leaned his cane against a tree and put on his tallis; his disciples did likewise. Around them, within them, the silence became more and more oppressive. Rabbi Yitzhak Hacohen and Rabbi Sasson found it difficult to control their emotions when the Maharal began to recite the first chapter of

Genesis, along with commentaries by our old sages. Insisting on the interpretation of the Zohar, whispering intensely, he evoked mysteries that men like him had conveyed to one another from generation to generation, from the time of Sinai and even from Creation. And beyond the silence, within the silence, the disciples heard voices rising and rising, higher and higher, from heaven to heaven, to become one with the Voice. And sud-

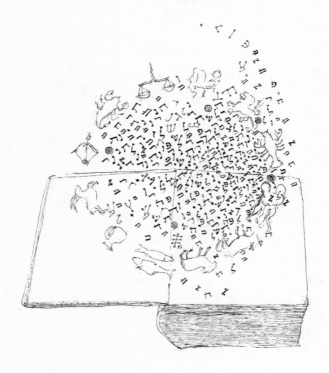

denly time stopped. The Maharal lit a torch and handed it to Rabbi Sasson, while he took his cane and drew a circle in the mud. Then he turned to his disciples and gave them precise instructions: Rabbi Yitzhak was to go around the drawing seven times, from right to left, starting at the feet, while softly repeating Names which, since the beginning of time, no human had the right to pronounce. Then it was the turn of Rabbi Sasson. And then the Maharal's. And then the torch went out by itself and, in the darkness, the two disciples thought they saw a hand, which began to draw a figure of clay. "Breathe," the Maharal said, leaning over the creature that was lying on the ground. And the man of clay began to breathe. "Open your eyes," said the Maharal. And the man of clay opened his eyes. "Sit up," the Maharal said. And the man of clay rose, slowly, heavily. "Stand," the Maharal told him. And the man of clay, with a jolt, stood up. "I name you Yoseph," said the Maharal. "Your mission on earth will be to protect the people of Israel from their enemies. Do you understand?"

The man of clay did not answer. "Yes, you do understand," the Maharal told him, "but you do not know how to express it; you will not be able to talk because that is a gift only God, blessed be His name, can give. In every other way you will be like us. Only more powerful. No one will be your match. You will conquer fire and death. As long as we need you, you will be indestructible and immortal.

From the bundle the Maharal had brought along, he pulled out garments and helped the Golem dress. "We will say that Yossel is my new beadle," explained the Maharal. "Born mute, he arrived in our midst as if from nowhere. That way the curious will not ask too many questions. What is the point of questioning someone who cannot answer? Come, my dear Yossel, let us go back."

Of course the Maharal was right. People quickly got used to seeing "Yossel the mute" move about in the shadow of the Master. The Golem would appear and disappear and only Rabbi Lowe knew why. No one but the Maharal had the right to give him orders or use his services. Those who did not follow the Maharal's exact instructions would regret it. Even the Rabbi's wife got herself into trouble. She asked the Golem to get some water from the well and to fill the barrel; he almost

caused a flood. Another time she asked him to catch a few fish for the Sabbath; he brought back hundreds. "Didn't I tell you to stay away from my Yossel?" said the Maharal. "He is here to serve me alone. I don't want to repeat this." Sometimes he gave him instructions through one of his two close disciples or through his servant, Reb Avraham Hayim. And even they were not to bother Yossel except as required by the needs and interest of the community.

Between Purim and Passover Yossel would wear Gentile clothes as he walked through the city's darkest streets. In spite of his exceptional strength, he would walk lightly, noiselessly. If he saw someone with a burden on his shoulder, or with a cart, he would stop him and subject him to a thorough search. At times, he would find a dead child, and then the Golem would tie the culprit to the child and bring him to the police.

When the Golem was not on a mission, he rested in his corner behind the hearth, in the darkest recess of the Rabbinical Court, as if he were hiding from visitors. But you only had to look at him to see that he filled the horizon.

Instinctively, people were reluctant to approach him. You could feel that he was someone apart; you could imagine he had a mysterious past. Was he a fool? A penitent? He behaved in a way that aroused talk and gossip: he did not attend services, never wore tefillin, never went to the Mikva. How could a Jew live like this, without following the commandments of the Torah? Here, too, people knew that there was no point in trying to understand: his case defied understanding.

Some loved him like a brother who has returned from far away and whom you cannot quite place. Others loved him as one loves a grown child. Some hated him, but he could not be attacked with impunity. A madman stared at him and started laughing noisily; the Golem lowered his head into his shoulders as if to become invisible. The madman touched him to provoke him and quickly pulled back his hand. "I am burning," he cried, "I am burning!" He died years later, screaming, "I am burning, I am burning!"

A nonbeliever made the mistake of hitting him: the Golem took the blows without complaining. His assailant continued to hit him: the Golem did nothing to resist. He let himself be beaten, staring dreamily into the void. Then suddenly the nonbeliever screamed; a moment later he lost his ability to speak.

But these were exceptional events. Usually the Golem lived apart, away from us, and only awoke when the Maharal sent him on a secret mission.

THE enemies of the Jewish people were also working in secret. One of them, a butcher by profession, had contracted a debt of five thousand crowns to the wealthy Rabbi Mordechai Meizel whose good deeds were legendary. The butcher, unable to meet his obligations, decided to get rid of his creditor by kidnapping his servant, Maria. Rabbi Mordechai was denounced to the authorities and put in chains, officially accused of sequestering or even murdering the Christian girl. Fear of further reprisals swept through our community. The inhabitants were afraid to go out on the streets: beggars avoided the city in spite of its beauty and warmth.

All sorts of memories surfaced. We had known enough pogroms to dread the outcome.

They would start with a speech or a rumor spreading throughout the Christian community, and end with mutilated bodies lying in front of our empty homes.

It was enough for a drunkard to accuse the Jews of poisoning a well or profaning the host, and peaceful neighbors would join the mob. We would lock our windows and doors, creep down into the cellar and try to disappear into the darkness. Outside, screams of vengeance from the mob; inside, the silence of Jewish prayers. I remember. I would feel like screaming, crying. I remember my father's hand held gently over my mouth.

But God protected us. This time, the storm passed quickly. After three days and three nights we felt secure enough to go back into our homes. The street was like a plowed-up cemetery; the houses of prayer plundered, desecrated, looted. I remember, and I'll remember until I die, sacred scrolls lying in the mud.

Oh yes, we knew that if our community was afraid, there was a reason. Were a tribunal to find Rabbi Mordechai Meizel guilty, it would have provoked a mass slaughter. The learned people quoted the scripture and its curses; we lived waiting for disaster. In the morning we would say, "May we see evening"; in the evening we would whisper, "May we see dawn."

But the Maharal, as usual, knew how to prevent catastrophe. The Jews gathered in the main synagogue to pray together. All eyes were turned to the empty seat next to the Maharal; its usual occupant, Rabbi Mordechai Meizel, imprisoned, charged with ritual murder, was undergoing endless torture. The Maharal was staring at the door. He had sent the Golem on a mission; he was waiting for his return. He should have been back two hours earlier; he wasn't usually late. The worried Maharal prayed, biting his lips.

During this time, the Golem—invisible—was searching every room of the Green Church, the official residence of the notorious Bishop Thadeusz. What was the Golem looking for? For Maria, the young woman who had disappeared.

"Yossel the mute" went from one room to another: nothing. He inspected the rooms in the cellar: no one. He was about to climb up to the steeple when he heard the sounds of a man crying softly, like a child. The Golem turned back and discovered a cell in a corner. Rabbi Mordechai, crouching on

the damp floor, his whole body covered with blood, was sobbing and groaning. The Golem could have picked him up and carried him away, but his mission was to find Maria, who in fact was locked up in the next cell. And there he found her, hurt but alive. Whom should he save? The Golem hesitated but an instant: he seized both of them, and a moment later they seemed to be floating in the air, above the town. He put them down into the street. Visible once more, he pushed them toward the synagogue, where they were greeted by an exuberant cry. They were surrounded, they were questioned, offered food and drink. As for the Maharal, he just whispered, "My dear little Yossel, thank you," and his smile became solemn. The Golem had found the culprit and the story ended happily.

In truth, all the stories of the "Golem made of clay" end well. They often begin in the same way: a Jew unjustly accused of imaginary crimes. They end in the same manner: the Golem intervening to put things in their proper place.

The Golem: servant and ally of the Maharal. It is the Maharal who understands and it is the Golem who acts. The intelligence of the former,

allied with the occult powers of the latter, never fails to arrive at the truth and therefore cause justice to triumph.

Their common enemy—the enemy of our entire community—was Bishop Thadeusz. This notorious character, a convert from Judaism, had a blind and all-encompassing hatred for the people he had repudiated. All he did was plot and agitate against the Jews, whom he wished to see massacred to the very last. From the Green Church he sent out his agents to spy on us, his lackeys to slander us and his mercenaries to attack us.

Sometimes through trickery he managed to lead a Jewish child away from his parents and his God, and to turn him against them.

For example, I remember a certain Gradowiczer . . . I have never seen a man so devastated. His daughter had deserted him following the evil advice of Thadeusz. She announced that she was ready to testify against Gradowiczer and to say that with her own eyes she had seen him pour Christian blood into the wine the night before the Seder. . . . The poor father, a widower, had brought up the daughter alone. He had sacrificed himself for her. He had abandoned his trade so that he could look after her. And now . . . But Thadeusz had not reckoned with the Maharal and the Golem. The young girl saw her dead mother in a dream. And the mother found the words to move her daughter to repentance. "I speak to you in the name of your ancestors," the mother told her. "They are all watching you. The happiness of your people, or whether they pass by the sword, depends on you: God Himself is watching you, my daughter. And so that you won't think that all this is just an empty dream, I will give you a sign: tomorrow, in your room, a man will rise up as if from nothingness. Do not speak to him; he is mute. His name is Yossel. . . ." Of course, the next day, making use of his gift of becoming invisible and then visible again, the Golem appeared in the girl's room.

And that same day, at the Court, in the presence of all the officials, instead of accusing her father, she told the truth about Thadeusz.

THADEUSZ, Thadeusz . . . No man was more wicked than he or more dangerous. He spent years and years of his life trying to harm the Jews of Prague, and, indeed, the Jews everywhere. In his hatred, he would spare no energy in forever searching for new ruses to entrap the faithful children, friends and associates, brothers and sisters. Were it not for the Maharal and the Golem . . .

Have I told you the story of Sophie? No? Well, let me tell it to you. I know, it has a familiar ring. But then, Thadeusz never hesitated to repeat an old trick. So, listen. Sophie was the breathtakingly beautiful daughter of a renowned physician. Intelligent, filled with curiosity, an eager reader of books of secular philosophy, Sophie saw no reason not to chat with one of her father's patients, a man

whom she often saw. He was a Christian—so what? Christians believe in God, do they not? He was a Bishop—so what? Titles have nothing to do with faith. So she allowed Thadeusz—yes, Thadeusz—to get her so confused that she decided to learn more about his religion; and then came to admire some of its customs; and then, finally, agreed to be baptized. I know, it is difficult to comprehend, but it happened: she abandoned her father, her family, her home, and ran away to Thadeusz's Green Church. . . . There the Bishop himself instructed her in all the lessons of catechism, and thus drew her farther and farther away from her people. He made her promise to prove her sincerity by turning against her own father; she was to swear before the Cardinal and the civil authorities that her father had murdered a Christian servant who had disappeared several weeks before. . . . Everything was ready. Satan above was anticipating the joy of mocking Israel's protective angels: the community of Prague was lost, yes, it was doomed; nothing could save it. Except that the Maharal and the Golem succeeded in tracking down the servant. And finding Sophie. Once again, the vile Thadeusz was defeated. Once again, Rabbi Lowe and "Yossel the mute" saved the life and the honor of the Jewish people. Have I not told you? When the Rabbi and the Golem joined forces, they were invincible.

They proved it on another occasion, one Passover, when the same wicked Thadeusz poisoned the Maharal's specially prepared—and rigorously supervised—matza shmura. How did the Maharal discover the plot? He was warned by a mistake in his Maariv prayer. He said "Umakhmitz" instead of "Umakhlif" *et hazmanim* . . . Blessed be the Lord who *sours*—and not, who *changes*—the seasons. . . . The Maharal stopped the service and ordered all the Jews to stay in their houses of prayer until his investigation was completed. He gave a piece of the matza to the Golem, who began to groan and moan: he was sick as never before.

The Maharal quickly established the fact that two Gentile apprentices called "redbeards" had helped bake the matza. They must have had something to do with the affair. But where does one get proof? The Maharal used his powers and made the Golem invisible. Thus Yossel could search their homes without being disturbed. And, of course, he discovered the poison. And naturally, the two

74

culprits were made to confess their crime. They named Thadeusz as the instigator. He had bought their services to poison the matza and bring disaster upon the entire community. This time, too, a miracle occurred, thank heaven, just in time to allow the community to celebrate Passover with joy.

Another story? Well, listen:

The Jewish families of our community used to talk about it. Everyone knew that it could have ended badly, but thanks to the great Maharal it brought us happiness. And glory.

It concerns an incredible adventure which takes place in more than one country and involves more than one Rabbi, and includes more than one miracle.

Once upon a time there was an extraordinary young Jewish woman named Reizel, wondrously beautiful, wise and devoted; whoever saw her could not help thanking God for having added beauty to His creation.

But it was exactly because she was more virtuous and intelligent than all her friends that Thadeusz decided to make her his prey and his evil tool. Ah, Thadeusz, Thadeusz, cursed be his name! In order to preach love for his God, he spread hatred for His people! If only you knew what he proposed to do with Reizel! Baptize her. If he had succeeded in his plans for her, he would have acquired such influence as to make the Jews tremble. . . . Everything was ready. So deeply was Reizel under Thadeusz's spell, that she agreed to meet him at a concert. There, to receive her, was a young duke, who, predictably, fell in love with her. Two dates were set: one for the baptismal ceremony and another for the wedding; all the noblemen and dignitaries of the kingdom were invited. But once again, Thadeusz hadn't taken the Maharal into account. Reizel's father, a merchant called Reb Mikhal Berger, had pleaded with the Maharal, and he had agreed to intervene and thwart the Bishop's plans. The Golem entered the confines of the convent as if it were his home, freed Reizel from her spell and led her far away to the other side of the mountains to Amsterdam where she had relatives. Years and years passed. The young duke could not forget his fiancée. He began to search for her throughout Europe, and particularly among Jews. In this way he discovered Jewish life, Jewish tradition, Jewish religion; in time he

was ready to study the Torah. Then, in spite of the Rabbis who tried to dissuade him—Judaism discourages conversion to the Jewish faith—he joined his fate to the fate of Israel. And after innumerable events, one stranger and more miraculous than the other, thanks to divine Providence, which presides over all human encounters, he found himself in the presence of a wonderfully beautiful and devout Jewish woman: the duke and Reizel were married according to the laws of Moses and Israel. Of course, Thadeusz, furious, sought revenge. He went so far as to hide the body of a Christian in the Maharal's own cellar. But the Golem discovered it and, according to Rabbi Lowe's wishes, took the corpse and put it in the Green Church. And the renegade, once more exposed and unmasked, confessed. Yes, not only was he involved in obstructing justice, but in an actual murder! The facts were irrefutable. He admitted it all in public.

Here then is the sad but shocking truth: this man who wanted to be a priest, and therefore a servant of God, had incited men and women to lie, to perjure themselves, to betray, to torture others, to jail them, to slaughter their children. He failed, and the threats were transformed into hope, and

פראג

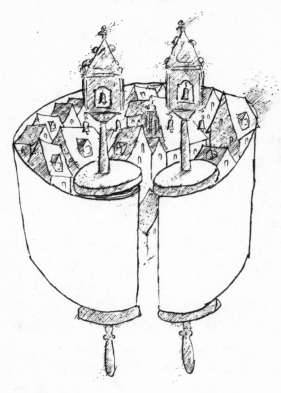

despair gave way to joy only because the great Maharal and his faithful companion the Golem knew how to interpret events and the people who tried to shape them. Without the Maharal and the Golem, the Jewish community of Prague might not have survived.

We cannot say often enough how much we owe them.

HE Maharal, humble but stubborn, allowed hardly any reference to his miraculous powers. His letters were signed simply, "Yehuda ben Bezalel"—son of Bezalel. After his death, out of respect for his wishes, the community omitted his titles from his tombstone. But we did believe in his miraculous powers. From the most ignorant to the wisest of our people, all were convinced that the Shekhina lived in our Master. He could see farther than anyone, and perhaps more than anyone; he ascended higher and his soul floated in the heavenly sphere inaccessible to common mortals. He was so pure that sin fled from him just as he fled from sin. Once, during a marriage ceremony, he was unable to bless the wine; the cup broke once, twice, three times. From above, he was being prevented from marrying a man and a woman who didn't know that they were in fact brother and sister. Another time he felt incapable of shaking hands with a visitor, even though the man was being honored everywhere for his generosity to the needy; what was not known was that the visitor was carrying on an adulterous relationship. Still another time, the Maharal wanted to visit the home of a scholar, but was unable to cross the threshold: the mistress of the house had unintentionally prepared nonkosher dishes.

Respected, admired by all, he used his authority to improve the lot of his brothers and sisters. The Cardinal took into account his advice about everything concerning the Jews of Prague. As did King Rudolph, who had become his friend since their encounter on the Charles Bridge. They would meet to study together. Or to be alone together. No one knows the questions they would ask of one another. But we do know that the king would often solicit his friend's advice. As a result, the Jews lived in peace, happy to be allowed to wait for the coming of the Messiah without fear of the fanatical plots of their enemies.

One day the two friends met by chance on the

street. The king stopped his carriage and told the Maharal to come closer. "Where are you going?" he asked, about to suggest that he take a seat next to him. "I don't know, Sire," answered the Maharal. "Are you making fun of your king? You don't know where you are going?" "No, I don't, your Majesty," replied the Maharal. Whereupon the king had him taken away to prison. The next day he was brought to the palace. "Why did you lie to me?" "I didn't lie, Sire. I really did not know where I was going. The proof: I was thinking of going to the synagogue and I landed in prison. . . ."

The king once tried to play a trick on him— without success. The story? The Maharal often dined with the king, but he always brought his own kosher plates and food. Once the ruler invited him out for a walk in the middle of a meal. In the meantime, the servants changed the Maharal's plate. When the Maharal and the king returned, the Maharal refused to touch his food although it "looked" kosher: he invoked an old custom that once one had risen from the table, one's food must not be eaten any more. Embarrassed and stunned, the king then confessed to his Jewish visitor that he had meant to test him. His admiration for the Maharal grew even more.

At another meeting, the king asked the Maharal to explain free choice: How can man be free when God knows in advance what he is going to do? "It is very simple," the Maharal said. "With your permission, we shall leave the city. Once outside, beyond the ramparts, I will predict which road your Majesty will take to come back. In this way, Sire, you will see for yourself that my foreknowledge will have no influence on your decision, which will still be free."

The king's horses were harnessed. Together, they left Prague. The Maharal wrote something on a piece of paper. The king took it, put it in an envelope and stamped it with a seal: it was not to be opened until the king returned.

Now, at that time, you could enter the city through four different gates. And, in order to confuse his Jewish friend, the king decided not to use any. He ordered a fifth one built. . . .

Unruffled, the Maharal waited until the king opened the envelope and read its contents: the Maharal had written a Talmudic saying: *Melekh poretz geder:* the king abolishes walls.

"You see, your Majesty," the Maharal told him. "You were free and yet our Sages knew. . . ." With this, their friendship grew even stronger.

AND the Golem, over the years, was less and less busy. No one came to disturb him any more. He spent his time sleeping or dreaming in his corner in the Rabbinical Court. Strangely enough, he did not eat, he did not drink —at least not in public. Another thing: he did not age. Time left no marks on his body. How did he manage this? No one knew. Everything about him was mysterious. And silent.

There were rumors that from time to time he became melancholy; his mouth would open and close as though he were trying to speak, his dark eyes turning darker, unfathomable. What was he thinking? He seemed to be calling someone; I wonder whom.

The Maharal came to visit him. The Golem   89

looked at him with sadness and shrugged his shoulders as if to indicate frustration.

Why this exhaustion—more exactly, this feeling of uselessness? Did he realize that he was no longer needed? That there was no longer any threat? That his life no longer mattered?

After a while, the Maharal acquired the habit of spending an hour or two with him every Friday afternoon, speaking to him softly. What did the Master discuss with his creature made of clay? It was said that he would tell him the story of Adam, whom the Lord brought into the world on Friday of the first week. Soon the Maharal too became dejected. Was it his age? His mystical adventures? He studied more than ever, exploring all aspects of Jewish life throughout all the kingdoms and the Holy Land. He spent entire days and nights writing. The future and the past, law and legend, messianic dreams and current realities: he was interested in everything and had his own opinion about everything. He saw fewer people. It was as if he knew that he did not have much more time; every moment was precious to him. But then, why did he devote so much time to the Golem? Who knows? Was it the bond the creator feels for his creation? Did he feel guilty for having brought him into the world?

I asked my father that question, but he only shook his head—it is dangerous to delve too deeply into the shadows. I insisted: in vain. Sometimes I would tell myself that the Maharal wanted to keep the Golem with him forever. Why not? Just as he knew how to create life, he could prolong it. Miracle? A word that means nothing. What is life if not a miracle? Two beings unite and enrich the world: isn't that a miracle? Or is it a miracle less spectacular than the one performed by the Maharal? I would have liked to hear the Golem's opinion.

TEN years after he was created, the Golem returned to dust. Here is how and under what circumstances. It was the 33rd day of Omer, in the year 5350 (or 1590 C.E.). The community evoked Rabbi Shimon bar Yohai, the disciples of Rabbi Akiba, the warriors of Betar; they cut the children's hair; they went into the woods to shoot arrows. As for the Maharal, he withdrew to his study. You could feel that he was meditating on serious matters.

That evening he summoned his two favorite disciples, Rabbi Yitzhak Hacohen and Rabbi Sasson, and announced his decision: Yossel's time had come. All three went to the Court. The Golem was dozing. When he saw the Maharal, his eyes seemed to light up. They darkened at the sight of

the disciples. "Yossel, my dear little Yossel," the Maharal said, and he began to choke. He could not go on. He started again, "My dear Yossel, listen." The Golem held his breath in order to listen better. "Tonight you will sleep somewhere else," the Maharal told him. He repeated, "Somewhere else, in the attic of the synagogue." The Golem bowed his head. He must have guessed the truth. Rabbi Yitzhak and Rabbi Sasson had tears in their eyes; so did the Maharal. "Come, my dear Yossel," he said. They went out into the night and walked in silence toward the synagogue. The Maharal climbed up to the attic and the Golem followed, with the two disciples close behind. For a moment the four remained completely motionless, as if glued to their own shadows. Then the voice of the Maharal broke the silence. "Lie down, dear little Yossel." The Golem hesitated imperceptibly before obeying. "Now, stretch out your arms," the Maharal said. The Golem stretched out his arms. "And your legs," the Maharal told him. The Golem stretched out his legs. "Lower your eyelids," said the Maharal. The Golem closed his eyes. "Breathe slowly, very slowly, slower and slower," the Maharal said. The Golem obeyed. "Do you feel sleep overtaking you?" asked the Maharal. The Golem wanted to nod his head to say yes, but his strength had left him. "You have accomplished your destiny," the Maharal said. "You can be proud. Few men have saved as many lives as you have. May your sleep be sweet, my dear Yossel; don't worry, no one will disturb you, I promise."

The Golem fell into a deep, endless sleep and the Maharal ordered his disciples to walk seven times around the body, but this time from left to right, starting at the head. It was the Master who led the way. He softly recited mystical formulas, ancient prayers dating back to the sixth day of creation; as for Rabbi Yitzhak and Rabbi Sasson, they were reciting psalms.

After the ceremony, the Maharal and his disciples took some old ritual vestments and covered the Golem from head to foot; when the tormented face of clay disappeared behind the torn tallis, the Maharal sighed mournfully.

The next day was a day without sun for the Jewish inhabitants of Prague.

The disappearance of the Golem did not create much of a stir. There was a rumor that "Yossel the mute," a vagrant by nature, had decided to go home, just like that, for no reason, without saying goodbye. Since people had never understood the Golem, they continued not to understand. After a few days, he was forgotten.

To maintain the mystery, the Maharal forbade, under threat of excommunication, any access to the attic of the synagogue. He gave no explanation other than that it would be dangerous. The people, used to obeying their Master, followed his will.

Shortly after the Maharal died, King Rudolph went mad and was forced to abdicate the throne. He spent the last years of his life obsessed with the health of his pet lion with whom, an astrologer once had told him, he shared a common horoscope.

It is said that, much later, someone opened the attic door of the Maharal's synagogue and glanced inside: he lost his sanity. Another lost his life. A third, his soul. And my father commented only: It is dangerous to look where you should not. But a wandering beggar whom I met recently gave me, under the seal of secrecy, his own explanation: the Maharal had forbidden access to the attic because, in truth, the Golem had remained alive. And he is waiting to be called.

As for me, I wish I knew.

GLOSSARY יהוה

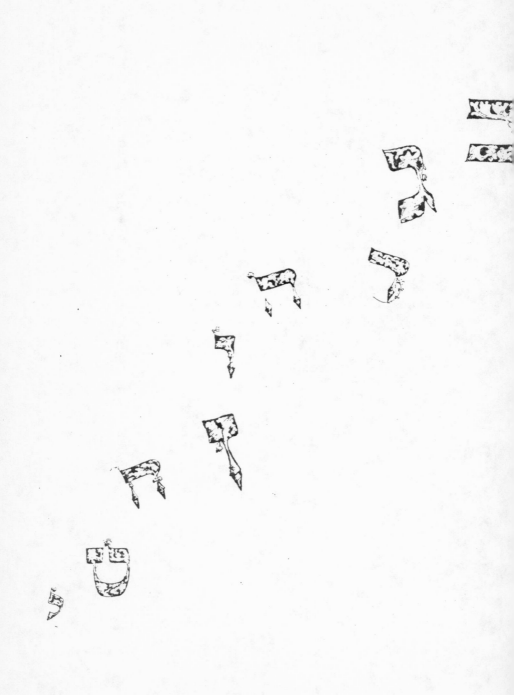

ADAR: Month in the Hebrew calendar falling in February-March.

ALEPH-BET: First and second letters of the Hebrew alphabet.

CANTOR: A synagogue official who sings or chants liturgical music and leads the congregation in prayer.

ELIJAH: The prophet who will come just before the Messiah and will blow his ram's horn to signal the Redemption and prepare the way for the Messiah. He has a special, symbolic place in the Passover seder—a cup of wine is set for him in the hope that he will appear.

GOLEM: In Jewish folklore, an artificial figure constructed to represent a human being and endowed with life.

THE HOLY BROTHERHOOD (sacred burial society): They perform rituals involved in the pre-burial purification of the body.

KABBALA: The Jewish mystical movement; the complex, esoteric body of Jewish mystical tradition, literature and thought.

103

KABBALIST: A Jewish mystic endowed with the ability to understand and interpret the lore of Kabbala, and having the power of divination.

MAARIV: Evening service (also called Arevit), recited daily after nightfall. It is named after one of the opening words of the first prayer.

MATZA SHMURA: The matza that is "watched" or "guarded" so that it does not become leavened. This especially "watched" matza (traditionally, from the time the wheat is cut) is usually served at the first seder.

MIDRASH: From a Hebrew verb meaning to expound, to interpret; specifically to expound the ethical directives of Scriptures. In fact, it is the large body of Talmudic literature that developed during the second century of the Common Era.

MIKVA: Ritual bath to wash away every uncleanness.

MINYAN: The ten male Jews required for religious services.

OMER: The sheaf of new barley traditionally brought to the Temple of Jerusalem as an offering on the second day of Passover.

PASSOVER: The deeply cherished eight-day Festival of Freedom that commemorates Israel's dramatic deliverance from enslavement in Egypt, as recounted in Exodus.

PURIM: The Feast of Lots, commemorating the rescue of the Jews of Persia from the wicked Haman, who plotted to exterminate every Jewish man, woman and child. It celebrates the heroism of Queen Esther and the wisdom of Mordecai, her uncle, both of whom effected the rescue. The Book of Esther tells the story.

RABBINICAL COURT: A rabbinical tribunal (beth din), usually consisting of three rabbis, that dealt with religious, domestic and business disputes. Those who came before it sought advice or arbitration. It had no legal authority, but many Jews preferred abiding by its decisions to seeking legal ones. Such tribunals, or courts, are still to be found in some religious communities.

RASHI: An acronym for Rabbi Isaac ben Shlomo, a scholar of eleventh-century France. His commentary on the Torah, a most important and widely studied work, is, by extension, also known as Rashi.

SEDER: The combination family feast and religious service, held on the two evenings before the first and second days of Passover, which is the highlight of this holiday. Seder means "order of procedure," and indeed an elaborate and symbolic ritual is carefully followed.

SHABBAT: The Sabbath, the weekly day of rest, observed from sunset of Friday to sunset of Saturday.

SHEKHINA: The Divine Presence. The radiance of the Shekhina with its many blessings accompanies those who are pious and righteous.

TALLIS: Prayer shawl.

TEFILLIN: Phylacteries—two leather cases containing paper inscribed with Scriptural writings, bound by straps attached to the forehead and the left arm during the morning prayer.

ZOHAR: The Book of Splendor, principal work of Kabbala.

ABOUT THE AUTHOR

ELIE WIESEL, author of twenty-one books, is University Professor and Andrew Mellon Professor in the Humanities at Boston University. He and his family live in New York City.

ABOUT THE ILLUSTRATOR

MARK PODWAL's drawings have been exhibited in many museums including the Louvre, the Musée des Beaux-Arts in Bordeaux and the Jewish Museum in New York.